Presented to:

_____

The date of:

_____

From:

_____

My Sleep-Tight Bible Stories

Written by

Jean Syswerda

Illustrated by

Jody Wheeler

Zonderkidz

MY SLEEP–TIGHT BIBLE STORIES
ISBN: 0-310-70174-0
Copyright © 2002 by Jean Syswerda
Illustrations © 2002 by Jody Wheeler

Zonder**kidz**™

The children's group of Zondervan

Requests for information should be addressed to:
Grand Rapids, Michigan 49530
www.zonderkidz.com

Published in association with the literary agency of Ann Spangler & Associates, 1420 Pontiac Road Southeast, Grand Rapids, Michigan 49506.

Zonderkidz is a trademark of Zondervan.

Edited by Gwen Ellis

Printed in China
01 02 03 04 05/HK/5 4 3 2 1

To Emelia Rae Grate.
May you sleep tight in Jesus all the nights of your life.
I love you!

— Grandma

For Sophie Greenwood, and new arrivals
Nora, Weston, and Clara

— J.W.

Introduction

One of the sweetest moments of the day is when you tuck your little ones—all clean and snuggly—into bed. That's the perfect time for this small book of bedtime stories that will not only teach your children the truths of God's Word, but will do it in a way that settles them down for sleep.

Some Ideas for Using My Sleep-Tight Bible Stories

★ Start by singing a quiet song.
★ As you read the story, notice the quiet scenes created, the gentle speech of the characters, and the positive character reinforcement that takes place.
★ Read just one story slowly in a soft and gentle voice.
★ Go over it several times and talk about it.
★ Do the "Tuck In" activity with your child.

Personalizing My Sleep-Tight Bible Stories

Every child likes to know he or she is very special, to you and to God. Take every opportunity to personalize the stories when possible. Here are some ideas:

★ Point out and talk about any part of the story with which your child can identify.
★ Use the "Tuck In" feature. It gives you something specific—often physical—to do with your child to make the story more personal. Use the child's name in prayer to help him or her become comfortable and intimate with God through prayer.
★ Snuggle with your child and look him or her in the eyes as you talk about the stories. The intimacy you establish with your child will form a foundation for his or her future intimacy with God.

There are many important elements involved in raising children. But nothing forms a better foundation for a future life as a believer than teaching your young children stories of God's Word and praying with them.

Adam & Eve's Garden Home

The sun went down behind the trees, and the sky turned pink and purple. The air grew cooler. Adam held Eve's hand as they took an evening walk through the garden. They watched a robin fluff her feathers and prepare to snuggle down for the night. A sleepy-eyed squirrel peeked out at them from his hole in a tree.

Soon God joined them on their walk. Adam and Eve walked and talked with God. They loved this quiet time with God as the sun set and the cool evening breezes began to blow. They were thankful to God for their beautiful garden home.

Then, the sky grew dark and one star after another appeared. Adam laid fresh leaves on the warm ground. He made a soft bed for Eve and himself. They lay down, closed their eyes, and quietly went to sleep in the safety of the garden. Good night, Adam. Good night, Eve.

Good night. Sleep tight.

..Tuck in . .

As you snuggle into your bed, thank God for the wonderful world he has made.

Noah's Rocking Boat

The ark rocked softly beneath Noah's feet. The rain had finally stopped, and the water was calm. It had rained for forty days and forty nights. But Noah and his family and the animals were safe and dry on their boat.

Every evening Noah carried a basket of hay to feed the animals. He didn't want them to feel hungry during the night. He fed some of the hay to the rabbits. He fed some of the hay to the deer. He patted the head of the cow as he walked past her pen. She mooed quietly when he left. Noah continued to walk along, passing the elephants and the sheep and the camels.

Noah stopped for a moment to watch as a mama kitty cuddled her sleeping babies. Then he walked into the small room where his wife was already asleep. Noah took off his sandals and lay quietly down next to her. He listened to her soft breathing, and he sighed. The creaking and rocking of the ark soothed Noah. Soon he, too, was asleep.

Good night, Noah. Good night. Sleep tight.

Tuck in

Pretend your bed is a softly rocking boat, and thank God for a warm and safe place to sleep.

Abraham & Sarah's Little Baby

Abraham lifted the flap of his tent and walked inside. He had been sitting outside, watching thousands of stars twinkling over his head. There were too many to even count.

Abraham watched as Sarah wrapped baby Isaac's blanket around him. Abraham touched Isaac's tiny nose with his

finger. Abraham and Sarah had waited so long for this baby. Finally their little boy had been born.

Sarah laid sleeping baby Isaac in his little bed. She leaned over to kiss him good night. Abraham hugged Sarah. The long day had tired both of them. They walked over to their blankets to go to sleep. A lamb outside the tent cried, "Baa-a-a." An owl hooted in the dark. Little Isaac sighed softly. With a prayer of thanks in their hearts, Abraham and Sarah both fell quietly asleep.

Good night, Abraham. Good night, Sarah.

Good night, baby Isaac.

Good night. Sleep tight.

Tuck in

Before you go to sleep, say a prayer and thank God for little babies.

Jacob Has a Dream

Jacob sat down and rested. He was on a trip and would be sleeping outside tonight. Jacob liked to sleep outside. He didn't have a pillow, so he found a smooth rock—just the right size—and rested his head on it. Jacob looked up. The moon hung huge and white in the sky. Its beams shimmered brightly down on him. Jacob smiled. Soon his eyes got heavy, then they closed, and he began to snore softly.

While he slept, Jacob had a dream. He saw a stairway that went from earth all the way up to heaven. Angels moved up and down it. At the top, Jacob saw God. God told Jacob that he would be with him wherever he went. God would always take care of Jacob.

Jacob woke up. What a wonderful dream! God was with him! Jacob turned over and closed his eyes again. The air was cooler now, so he pulled his arms inside his robe. He felt warm and safe and comfortable. Soon Jacob was sleeping again.

Good night, Jacob. Good night. Sleep tight.

Tuck in

Ask God to give you good dreams as you go to sleep tonight.

Joseph Forgives His Brothers

Joseph squeezed his eyes shut then opened them again. He couldn't believe what he was seeing. His brothers knelt in front of him. But they didn't know he was their brother. They thought he was an Egyptian ruler. They had sold Joseph into slavery many years before, and they weren't sure he was even alive anymore.

As Joseph looked at his brothers' faces, he didn't feel angry or hurt or upset. He only felt thankful that he had a chance to see them again.

Joseph squeezed his eyes shut again. This time he was trying to keep the tears from coming. But he couldn't stop them. With a cry, he went to each brother and lifted him up. Reuben! Judah! Simeon! Benjamin!

Joseph's brothers weren't sure they could believe what was happening. Here was Joseph. And he wasn't angry with them. He forgave them for what they had done!

That night the brothers talked quietly for a long time in their bedroom in Joseph's huge palace. Then one, then another, grew quiet and fell asleep. They were thankful and happy that Joseph still loved them and forgave them. In his own room, Joseph slept quietly; glad his brothers were with him.

Good night, Joseph. Good night, Joseph's brothers.
Good night. Sleep tight.

Tuck in

Go to sleep tonight and be thankful for your brothers and sisters and friends.

Baby Moses in His Basket

A basket bobbed slowly up and down, up and down on the river. Inside was a sweet little baby boy. His name was Moses. A bad king wanted to hurt baby Moses. So his mother made a little basket and put him in it. She hid him in the plants that grew along the river.

After a while, little Moses got hungry. He started to cry as the basket floated down the river. A princess was taking a bath in the river. She heard Moses crying, and she felt sorry for him. She took him out of his basket and held him close. Baby Moses stopped crying when the princess held him close.

The princess looked for someone to help. Moses' sister, Miriam, ran up to the princess. She told the princess that her mother would take care of the baby. So the princess sent Miriam to get her mother! As soon as their mother arrived, she picked up baby Moses and held him tight. Baby Moses fell sound asleep in her arms. Baby Moses fell asleep as soon as his mother held him tight in her arms.

Good night, Moses. Good night. Sleep tight.

Tuck in

Cuddle up close to someone tonight and thank God that he takes care of you.

A Little Israelite Girl Crosses the Red Sea

It had been a big day for the Israelites and for one little Israelite girl. Everyone felt tired. Some people yawned. Others rubbed their eyes. Little children fussed.

The little girl and her family and hundreds of other Israelites had finally left Egypt. They had been slaves there. Now they were free. But they were also afraid. The huge Red

Sea lay in front of them. They didn't know how they would get across.

But God came and drove the water up into huge banks. The little girl and the rest of the Israelites walked right through on dry ground. Holding her mother's hand, the little girl looked to her right and to her left. She and her mother smiled at each other and at the sturdy walls of water.

Then, when everyone had crossed to the other side of the Red Sea the people lay down under the stars and fell right to sleep. The little Israelite girl curled up next to her mother. She felt her mother's warm arm around her. She felt safe because her mother was there and God was taking care of them.

Good night, little Israelite girl.

Good night. Sleep tight.

Tuck in
Thank God for keeping you safe as you sleep tonight.

A Little Israelite Boy Eats Manna

What a funny breakfast the little Israelite boy's mother served him this morning. Then, she served the same thing for lunch. And for supper! She had found the manna on the ground that morning. She told her son that the manna was special food from God. It crunched in the little boy's mouth. It tasted so good, like crackers sweetened with honey. Yummy!

The Israelites were in the desert. The ground was hard and dry. No food grew there. So God sent manna to feed his people while they traveled in the desert.

The little boy's tummy was full. He was getting sleepy. With a smile, he lay down and covered himself with his robe. He was thinking about the next morning, when there would be more manna on the ground. He closed his eyes and was soon fast asleep.

Good night, little Israelite boy.

Good night. Sleep tight.

Tuck in

Before you go to sleep tonight, thank God for the good food
you have to eat.

Joshua and the Walls of Jericho

Joshua remembered the first time he had seen the high and thick walls of Jericho. He had to bend his neck way back just to see the top! How would he and the Israelites ever get inside?

God told Joshua what to do. He and his soldiers and priests walked around the walls of Jericho once every day for six days. On the seventh day, they walked around the walls one, two, three, four, five, six, seven times. Then the priests blew their trumpets. The soldiers shouted. And the mighty walls of Jericho fell down, just as God said they would. Boom! Crash!

Today had been a great victory for God and for the Israelites. Joshua went into his tent and lay down. He had never felt so tired. But he was excited too. He could still hear some of the people outside laughing and talking and praising God. Joshua thanked God for the victory. And very soon he slept.

Good night, Joshua. Good night. Sleep tight.

...Tuck in...

Ask God to show you what to do, like Joshua did.

Samson

Samson ran his hand over the short hairs on his head. While he was sleeping the night before, some soldiers had cut off the seven braids of his long hair. When his hair was cut, Samson's amazing strength left him. Samson was sad. He was not strong anymore.

Samson had thought he was strong because he had big muscles. But now he knew the truth. His strength hadn't come from his big muscles. His strength had come from God.

Samson was sorry for thinking he was strong on his own. He prayed and asked God to forgive him. He asked God to make him strong again. Samson's hair began to grow back. God would make him strong again.

Samson lay down on his mat and closed his eyes. Soon he was asleep.

Good night, Samson. Good night. Sleep tight.

Tuck in

Stretch out your arms and legs, and thank God for making you strong.

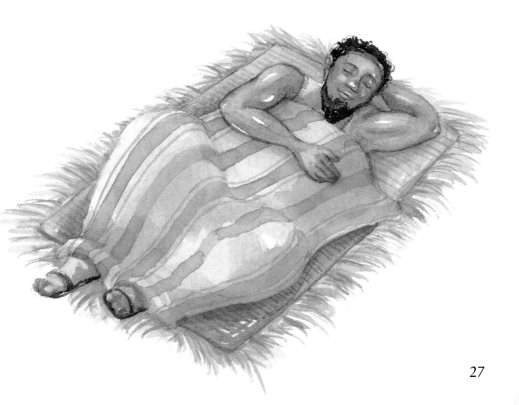

Naomi & Ruth Walk to Bethlehem

Naomi leaned over and sighed. "I'm so tired," she said to Ruth. "I can't go one more step."

Ruth smiled tiredly at Naomi. "I'm tired, too, Naomi," she agreed. Ruth put her hand over her mouth as she yawned. She reached down to rub her sore leg.

Naomi and Ruth were walking from Moab to Bethlehem. It was a long and hard trip. Naomi thought Ruth should stay with her family in Moab. But Ruth wanted to go to Bethlehem with Naomi.

Ruth knew Naomi was too tired to go on. "I see a big tree and some grass ahead, Naomi. We can rest there tonight."

Naomi smiled at Ruth. Since Naomi was old, she was so glad to have the young woman with her. They were hoping life in Bethlehem would be better for them. They didn't know it yet, but God had wonderful things planned for them—a husband for Ruth and children and contentment.

Naomi and Ruth sat down in the cool shade of the tree. Ruth got out some bread and cheese for their supper.

Later Ruth took out an extra blanket and put it over the sleeping Naomi. Soon Ruth lay down too. The grass felt soft and cool. Soon Ruth's eyes closed, and she slept.

Good night, Naomi. Good night, Ruth.

Good night. Sleep tight.

Tuck in

Pretend your bed is in soft green grass. Snuggle down and thank God for taking care of you.

Hannah's Baby Boy

Hannah rubbed her cheek against baby Samuel's soft head. She loved the feel of his smooth skin. She loved his warm baby smell. She had prayed so long to have a baby! Now God had answered her prayer.

Hannah prayed and thanked God for little Samuel. She asked God to help her to be a good mother. Hannah told God she would never forget that little Samuel was a gift from God.

A cool breeze ruffled Hannah's hair as she lay next to Samuel. She wanted to be close to him during the night. When he woke up crying and hungry, she would be right there.

Hannah closed her eyes and sighed. She felt warm and happy. Soon she would be sleeping just as little Samuel slept.

Good night, Hannah. Good night, Samuel.

Good night. Sleep tight.

Tuck in
Cuddle in bed with your mom or dad or brother or sister.
Before your sleep, thank God for your family.

God Talks with Samuel

Young Samuel lay sleeping in his bed in the tabernacle. His eyes flew open when he heard someone calling him.

"Samuel!"

Who was that? Samuel padded off with bare feet and went to Eli the priest's bed.

"Here I am. Did you call me?" he asked.

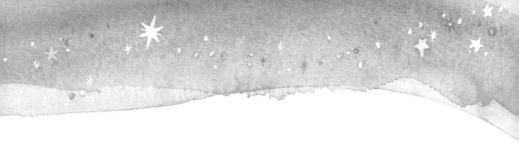

But Eli said, "No, I didn't call you."

Samuel heard the voice two more time. And two more times he went to Eli. Finally Eli told Samuel what to say the next time he heard the voice calling his name.

Samuel went back and climbed into his bed. This time, he hadn't even closed his eyes before he heard it. "Samuel!"

Samuel now knew it was God calling him. So he answered as Eli had told him. "I'm listening, Lord." The Lord told Samuel that he had a very special work for him to do.

Samuel didn't think he would be able to go back to sleep after talking with God. But soon his eyes were closed, and he was snoring softly.

Good night, Samuel.   Good night, Eli.

Good night. Sleep tight.

Tuck in
Be sure to talk with God tonight before you go to sleep.

David Sings and Sleeps

David shifted restlessly in the grass. The sky above him was full of stars. There were so many stars that he couldn't begin to count them. He looked out at the sheep. They didn't seem to have a problem sleeping. Even the bouncy, busy little lambs were now quiet and peaceful.

David turned and pulled his coat more closely around him. He closed his eyes and tried to keep them closed. But they just kept popping open. He couldn't fall asleep.

Finally, David gave up. He sat up and reached for his harp. He never went anywhere without his harp. Closing his eyes, David began to play and sing. He started with his favorite song. The song praised God for the beautiful world he had made. David sang and played quietly for a long time.

Later David realized he had fallen asleep with his harp in his hands. He put it down and lay in the soft grass. Soon he was sleeping as peacefully as the sheep around him.

Good night, sheep. Good night, David.

Good night. Sleep tight.

Tuck in

Quietly sing a song to God before you go to sleep tonight.

Wise King Solomon

Solomon was a great and mighty king. He wore a big gold crown and sat on a beautiful throne.

One night Solomon had a dream. God told Solomon he would give him whatever he asked for. Solomon thought and thought. What should I ask for? A new crown? A new palace? A new chariot? Then Solomon decided. He knew what he needed most of all. Solomon chose to ask for wisdom. He needed wisdom more than anything else God could give him.

God was pleased with Solomon. He said he would make Solomon the wisest king who ever lived. God said he would make Solomon very rich and let him live a long life too! Solomon woke up. He knew God had come to him in his dream.

Solomon's dream came true. He became the wisest king who ever lived. He was very rich, and he was king over Israel for forty years.

It was a long time that night before Solomon could sleep again. But just before the sun rose, a snore came from his mouth. Shhhhh! Solomon is sleeping.

Good night, King Solomon.

Good night. Sleep tight.

Tuck in
Ask God to help you sleep well and to make you wise as you grow up.

Josiah

Josiah lay in his bed with his eyes closed. But he wasn't sleeping. He opened his eyes. Josiah could see his new crown on the low table next to him. The gold in the crown sparkled in the moonlight.

Today had been a very busy day. Today Josiah had been crowned king of all Israel. And Josiah was only eight years old! Josiah thought about the sound of the music—harps and drums and trumpets and singers. The people had shouted loudly when the crown had been placed on his head. He remembered how heavy the golden crown felt on his head.

Josiah loved God very much. He wanted to do what was right. He also knew he was very young. But he decided he would follow God all his life. He knew he needed God's help for the work ahead. He thought about a wise man that he knew. The wise man would teach him how to be a good king.

Josiah burrowed down into his blankets and closed his eyes again. This time they stayed closed. Soon he was sound asleep.

Good night, young King Josiah.

Good night. Sleep tight.

Tuck in

Be like young Josiah tonight, and decide in your heart to follow
God all the days of your life.

39

Elijah

Elijah was hungry. His tummy went r-r-r-rumble and gr-r-r-rumble. He needed something to eat. God told Elijah to go to a nearby stream. God would make sure Elijah had enough to eat.

Elijah went to the stream. He splashed some water on his face and took a drink. The water tasted cool and refreshing. Then Elijah looked around. He didn't see any food anywhere. He trusted that God would take care of him. But he wondered how.

Late in the evening, God sent some birds to the stream. They whooshed down out of the sky and landed near Elijah.

Some of them dropped bread. Others dropped meat. Instead of eating the food themselves, the birds whooshed back up into the sky and flew away. Elijah picked up the food and ate it. Every morning and every night, the birds came and brought food to Elijah. God said he would take care of Elijah. And he did.

Elijah's tummy wasn't r-r-r-rumbling and gr-r-r-rumbling anymore. He felt full and satisfied. He felt glad because he knew God was taking care of him. Elijah lay down in the warm grass near the stream. He listened to the wind whistle through the trees over his head. He watched the stars come out one by one. Soon his eyes slipped shut, and with a happy sigh, he went to sleep. Good night, Elijah. Good night. Sleep tight.

Tuck in
Thank God for taking care of you and making sure you have enough to eat.

Elisha

Elisha sat down on the chair in his new room. He took off his sandals. Then he went to his bed and lay down. The blankets felt soft and new. A man and his wife had built this room just for him!

How kind the man and his wife were to make Elisha feel so comfortable. Elisha thanked God for them. And he wondered what he could do to thank them.

God let Elisha know a secret. The woman didn't have any children. She wanted to have a baby. Now Elisha knew what God wanted him to do. Elisha called to the woman and said, "Next year you will have a son to hold in your arms."

The woman wondered to herself, *Could this really happen?*

It did happen, just as God said it would. A year later the woman had a baby. She held and cuddled him in her arms. She trailed her finger gently along his baby cheek to make him smile. She was so happy.

Elisha looked around at the new walls, the new lamp, the new chair, and table. He sank into the comfortable bed.

He thanked God for keeping his promises. Then he closed his eyes and quickly went to sleep.

Good night, Elijah. Good night. Sleep tight.

Tuck in

Before you close your eyes and go to sleep, thank God for always keeping his promises.

Daniel

R-r-r-oarrrr!

The lions roared at Daniel. Daniel was in a den of lions. He had obeyed God instead of the king. The king said Daniel should pray to him. Daniel knew that was wrong. He kept praying to God instead. So the king put Daniel in the lions' den.

Daniel turned and looked at the lions. Big ones. Small ones. The big lions had big roars. The little lions had little

roars. But they didn't hurt Daniel. And they stopped roaring at him. God had sent his angel to protect Daniel. As soon as the lions saw the angel, they stopped their big and little roars. They closed their eyes and went to sleep, just like little kittens.

Daniel watched the lions as one by one they closed their mouths. Then one by one they closed their eyes! Then one by one they went to sleep! The lions were not even interested in hurting him. God was protecting his servant Daniel.

Daniel sat down against the wall. He knew God was with him, so he wasn't afraid. His eyes closed. Soon Daniel was sleeping, just like the lions.

Good night, Daniel.

Good night. Sleep tight.

Tuck in

Are you ever afraid? Of course, you are! Ask God to be with you and keep you safe, just like he was with Daniel.

Jonah's Ride in a Fish

Jonah tumbled and rolled and flipped and flopped and came to rest on a sandy beach. He let out a big sigh and then sat up to look around. He was out of the fish and on dry land again. Now Jonah knew exactly what he had to do. He had to go to Nineveh.

God had told Jonah to go to Nineveh to tell the people there about God. But Jonah didn't want to go. So he got into a boat that was sailing in the opposite direction. When a huge storm came up, Jonah knew God had sent it. He told the sailors to throw him overboard to stop the storm. They didn't

want to do it, but finally it seemed like they had no choice. The boat was going to sink if they didn't do something fast! So they tossed Jonah into the water.

That is when the big fish swallowed Jonah. He spent three days in the fish's stomach. God had sent the fish to save Jonah. He still wanted Jonah to go to Nineveh. So he told the fish to spit Jonah out onto the beach.

Jonah picked a piece of seaweed off of his shoulder. He shook sand out of his robe. Then he stood up. He needed to get going to Nineveh! But first he needed to rest. On shaky legs, Jonah walked toward some grass and trees. When he got there, he lay down. He curled up and quickly fell asleep.

Good night, Jonah. Good night. Sleep tight.

Tuck in
Before you go to sleep tonight, ask God to help you always obey him.

Nehemiah Builds a Wall

Today had been a big day for Nehemiah and the people of Judah. They had finished building a new wall around Jerusalem. Today they had a party to celebrate. Two choirs walked on the wall and sang. The priests played their trumpets and some of the other people played their harps and cymbals. The people shouted for joy. They thanked God for helping them finish the wall.

Nehemiah smiled to himself as he remembered the special day. He looked out his window. In the moonlight he could see a part of the wall of Jerusalem. It looked beautiful to him. He and the people had worked hard to rebuild the wall. Now they felt safe. And they knew God would bless them if they obeyed him.

Nehemiah lay down on his bed. He was tired and ready for sleep. But before he closed his eyes, he thanked God once more for the special day. He thanked God for helping him and the people of Judah. Then he closed his eyes and went to sleep.

Good night, Nehemiah. Good night. Sleep tight.

Tuck in

As you snuggle down to sleep, thank God for helping you and your family.

49

Baby Jesus Is Born

Mary carefully wrapped her little baby in soft blankets. She pulled them snug around him, so he would feel safe and secure. She softly kissed his smooth cheek. She touched his tiny fingers. Then she sat back and held him close to her. She quietly sang a song to her baby. Her mother had sung the same song to her when she was little. The cows moo-o-o-ed along. The sheep ba-a-a-ed quietly. Baby Jesus had been born in a stable!

Mary looked up and saw Joseph smiling at her. They both knew their baby was someone special. He was Jesus! He had come to earth for a very special purpose. When he grew up, he would be the Savior of the world. People had been waiting for him for a long time. Finally Jesus had come.

Mary continued to sing softly. She rocked baby Jesus in her arms, and before long he slept soundly. Mary laid him down in the hay. Mary lovingly touched baby Jesus' small face one more time. Then she lay in the hay next to him and went to sleep. Good night, Mary. Good night, baby Jesus. Good night. Sleep tight.

Tuck in

Tonight thank Jesus that he came to earth as a baby and grew up to be our Savior.

The Shepherds See Baby Jesus

The shepherds sat under the stars watching their sheep. They watched to be sure that no little lamb ran away. They watched to be sure that nothing hurt their sheep.

Suddenly, an angel appeared right in front of the shepherds. The angel was bright and huge. The shepherds had never seen an angel before. They were so scared! But the angel told them not to be afraid. He said that he had good news for them. Baby Jesus had been born in Bethlehem! The angel was then joined by thousands of angels. They all sang together and praised God.

When the angels went away, the shepherds decided they wanted to see this baby Jesus. They went to Bethlehem and found him sleeping in the hay, just as the angels said they would. They praised God for baby Jesus.

Then the shepherds went back to their sheep. They were still praising God. They talked and laughed and smiled at each other. Then, slowly, they began to settle down. One by one, the shepherds fell asleep.

Good night, shepherds. Good night. Sleep tight.

Tuck in

Before you go to sleep tonight, praise God for baby Jesus.

Jesus Takes a Boat Ride

One day Jesus and his disciples went for a ride in a boat. The boat gently rocked and swayed in the water. The wind began to blow. The boat rocked and swayed harder. The disciples thought the boat might tip over! They wanted Jesus to help them, but he was taking a nap.

When the disciples woke Jesus up, he felt the wind and the rocking boat. He heard the disciples asking him for help. Jesus held up his hands and scolded the wind and waves. He told them, "Be still!" Right away, the wind stopped and the waves calmed down and the boat stopped rocking. The disciples were amazed at Jesus' power.

Jesus loved his disciples. He was surprised that they were afraid. Didn't they know they were safe with him? He went back to his place in the boat and fell back to sleep.

Good night, Jesus. Good night. Sleep tight.

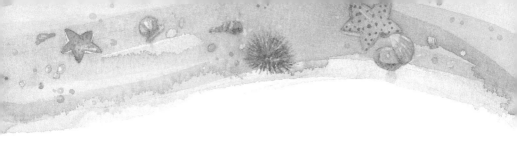

Tuck in

As you go to sleep in your soft bed, remember that Jesus is with you and you are safe.

The Disciples and a Little Lunch

It had been a very busy day for Jesus' disciples. Many people had been with them all day. Jesus healed the sick people. The little children sat on his lap. Jesus told them stories about God.

Late in the day, the people started to get hungry. But there wasn't very much food. A little boy had five loaves and two fish. Jesus took that little lunch and made it enough to feed all the people. It was amazing and exciting! Everyone had enough to eat. And there were even some pieces of bread and fish left over. The disciples went through the crowd and put all the leftover pieces in baskets.

The sun sank low in the sky, and most of the people went home to sleep. Jesus and his disciples were tired too. They found a grassy hill by the lake and sat down, talking quietly together. A breeze from the lake cooled them. One, two, three, four, five, six, seven, eight, nine, ten, eleven, twelve—soon all of Jesus' disciples were sleeping.

Good night, disciples. Good night. Sleep tight.

Tuck in

Thank Jesus for the good food you have to eat each day.

The Lost Son Comes Home

The son who had been lost rested on the clean, soft blankets of his bed. He had been gone for a long time, but now he was home again. And it felt wonderful.

When the son had left a long time ago, he wanted his share of money. He wanted to live on his own. Then he spent all the money and had nothing. He thought that perhaps his father wouldn't welcome him home. But as he walked down the road toward home, his father saw him coming and ran to meet him. Instead of scolding him or turning him away, his father hugged and kissed him.

A big welcome-home party was held that night. All the neighbors came with lots of good food and music and laughter. The lost son enjoyed the party. But more than anything, he enjoyed seeing his father again and knowing his father still loved him.

The lost son held up his hand to look at the new ring on his finger. His father had given it to him. He looked at the rich new robe that hung on a hook in his room. His father had given him that too. How glad the father was to see his son! And how glad the son was to see his father!

With a sigh and a smile, the lost son turned over on his blankets. He wasn't lost anymore. For the first time in a long time, he fell asleep, happy and contented.

Good night, my son. Good night. Sleep tight.

Tuck in
As you lie in your bed, thank God for your home and your mommy and daddy.

Eutychus Falls Out the Window

Eutychus climbed the stairs to the room where Paul was speaking. Up, up, up, he climbed. He wanted to hear this man who would tell him about Jesus.

It was late at night and already dark outside. Many lamps were burning in the room. It was very bright and very warm. Eutychus looked across the room and saw a window. He could sit there. He would be cooler there.

Eutychus listened to Paul tell about Jesus. Paul kept talking and talking. Eutychus kept listening. But he was starting to get very sleepy. He tried to keep his eyes open, but he just couldn't. Soon he was asleep in the window. And then he fell out the window! Down, down, down, boom! Eutychus fell onto the ground. He hit so hard he died.

The people in the room all jumped up. Paul ran down the stairs to where Eutychus lay on the ground. Paul put his arms around him and hugged him. Eutychus came back to life! The people knew they had seen something amazing.

Eutychus was thankful to God for all that had happened. Paul preached all night long, but the next night when he fell asleep, it was in his bed instead of a window.

Good night, Eutychus. Good night. Sleep tight.

Tuck in
Thank God for a warm and soft bed to sleep in.

Paul Sings in Jail

Paul was in jail. And he hadn't even done anything wrong! Instead of obeying some leaders of the land, Paul had obeyed God. Now he was being punished. He was tired and sore. But he didn't cry or moan or yell. Instead, Paul began to sing! Paul sang happy songs that praised God.

First, he sang softly. Then, he began to sing louder. His friend Silas joined in. Their voices echoed off the stone walls of the prison. Soon the other prisoners were lifting their heads and listening. They hadn't heard such a happy sound in a long time. They smiled and enjoyed the singing. Some of them even began to sing along. The jail rang with their voices. Up in heaven, God smiled when he heard their praises.

Then God sent an earthquake that opened all the prison doors. The jailer came to see what had happened. He felt so sorry for Paul; he took Paul to his house. The jailer gave him food and medicine. Then Paul told all the people God loved them. They gave their hearts to Jesus. After a while it was time for Paul to go to sleep. It had been a very long day. He closed his eyes. Soon he was snoring.

Good night, Paul. Good night. Sleep tight.

Tuck in

Sing one soft and one loud song of praise to God before you go to sleep tonight.

Good night, little one. Good night. Sleep tight.